BLOODLINES

FIGHTING PHANTOMS

written by
M. Zachary Sherman

illustrated by
Fritz Casas

colored by
Marlon Ilagan

STONE ARCH BOOKS
a capstone imprint

DEDICATED TO THE MEN AND WOMEN
OF THE ARMED SERVICES

Bloodlines is published by Stone Arch Books,
a Capstone imprint, 151 Good Counsel Drive,
P.O. Box 669 Mankato, Minnesota 56002
www.capstonepub.com Copyright © 2011 by
Stone Arch Books All rights reserved. No
part of this publication may be reproduced
in whole or in part, or stored in a retrieval
system, or transmitted in any form or by any
means, electronic, mechanical, photocopying,
recording, or otherwise, without written
permission of the publisher.

Cataloging-in-Publication Data is available on
the Library of Congress website.
ISBN: 978-1-4342-2560-3 (library binding)
ISBN: 978-1-4342-3099-7 (paperback)

Summary: In late 1970, Lieutenant Verner
"Hershey" Donovan sits aboard the USS
Constellation aircraft carrier, waiting to fly
his F-4 Phantom II over the skies of Vietnam.
He's the lead roll for the next hop and eager
to help the U.S. troops already on the ground.
Then suddenly, the call comes in — a Marine
Recon unit has taken heavy fire and requires
air support. Within moments, Donvan and
the other pilots are into their birds and into
the skies. Soon, however, a dogfight with MiG
fighter planes takes a turn for the worse, and
the lieutenant ejects over enemy territory. His
co-pilot is injured in the fall, and Donovan must
make a difficult choice. In order to save his
friend, he must first leave him behind.

Art Director: Bob Lentz
Graphic Designer: Brann Garvey
Production Specialist: Michelle Biedscheid

Photo credits: Alamy: Hannu Mononen, 35;
Corbis: Bettmann, 68, 69; Corel, 49; Getty
Images Inc.: AFP/STF, 7; Shutterstock: Jackson
Gee, 48, JustASC, 83; U.S. Air Force photo, 25,
34; U.S. Navy photo, 24, PH3 Marquart, 82

Printed in the United States of America
in Stevens Point, Wisconsin
092010   005934WZS11

TABLE OF CONTENTS

PERSONNEL FILE

Lieutenant
VERNER DONOVAN

ORGANIZATION:
VF-96 squadron, U.S. Navy

ENTERED SERVICE AT:
Camp Pendleton, CA

BORN:
November 7, 1951

EQUIPMENT

- SPH-4 Flight Helmet
- Dog Tags
- Life Preserver Vest
- Ammo Belt
- Flight Suit
- First-Aid Pouch
- .45 Caliber Pistol
- Survival Knife

OVERVIEW: VIETNAM WAR

The Vietnam War began as a conflict over what kind of government the country would have: communist or capitalist. At the start of the war in 1959, South Vietnam and North Vietnam were two separate countries. South Vietnam battled the communist Vietcong of the South and the communists of North Vietnam. The Vietcong and North Vietnam wanted to unite the two countries into one communist nation. They were backed by the Soviet Union and China. Under the leadership of President Lyndon Johnson, the United States supported South Vietnam with money and troops.

PRESIDENT JOHNSON

MAP

Dong Hoi

DMZ

VIETNAM

Da Nang

THAILAND

LAOS

Phu Cat

CAMBODIA

Pleiku

Phnom Penh

Cam Ranh

GULF OF THAILAND

Saigon

SOUTH CHINA SEA

MISSION

When the Marine Recon unit Razor Two takes heavy fire on the ground in Vietnam, the VF-96 "Fighting Falcons" squadron must provide air support.

CHAPTER 001

THE LAUNCH

Lieutenant Verner "Candy Man" Donovan unwrapped silver foil from around a tear-dropped bit of chocolate. He popped it in his mouth. Then he turned and laughed at his radar intercept officer, who really didn't like being in the Navy.

"I'm just sayin' it's a job, not an adventure," said Lieutenant Bobby "Blam" Hassleback. The young recruit shifted in the back seat, doing his best not to ruin the latest copy of the *Amazing Illusions* comic clutched in his hands. "Especially given the cramped quarters."

Blam was right. The cockpit of an F-4 Phantom II was definitely cramped. They were a two-man flight crew, pilot and RIO, strapped into the front nose cone of a 60,000-pound fighter jet. While in the cockpits of their planes, the men that flew in the VF-96 "Fighting Falcons" squadron from the deck of the CVA-64 USS *Constellation* aircraft carrier were gods among men.

They were masters of flying these two-man wrecking machines. They commanded jets that carried 5000-pound bombs, thousands of rounds of ammunition, and air-to-air missiles. The Fighting Falcons could attack a target and disappear into the clouds before the enemy even knew what hit them. They were phantoms.

Donovan's F-4 was parked in a Ready-Five formation on the carrier's deck. It was locked onto the steam-driven catapult and primed for launch. He could take off and be in the sky, ready for battle, in less than five minutes. The anticipation was nerve-racking, and the men did what they could to avoid focusing on it. In this case, Blam read comics, and "Candy Man" Donovan ate chocolates.

"It's not like you were drafted, Blam, you volunteered for this," Donovan said, licking caramel off his teeth.

"Yeah, for college credit," Blam replied. "Not for getting my *butt* shot out of the sky!"

Blam chuckled as Donovan's eyes glanced back at him from the jet's small rearview mirror. They were strapped so tightly into their ejection seats it was difficult for Donovan to turn around and glare at him.

"And what did you think a radio intercept officer was, anyway?" Donovan asked.

"You know, a radar man!" said Blam. "A guy that sits in an air-conditioned room all day and says, 'Look out, plane to your left!'"

Donovan shook his head. He adjusted the ear pad on his flight helmet. Each of their helmets were standard-issue gear. However, pilots and their crew were encouraged to decorate them any way they saw fit. Donovan's was painted chocolate brown with gold and purple stripes. Swirls of gold reflective tape adorned the sides. Above his visor control knob, in small white press-on letters, CANDY MAN was taped. This was Donovan's call sign, a nickname given to him because of his love for sweet treats.

Blam's helmet, on the other hand, was bright yellow with white starbursts. His call sign, BLAM, was also taped above his visor. Many people thought he had gotten the name because he was an amazing fighter, but it was really given to him because of his love for comic books. He always had one with him.

Radio traffic filled their headsets as the control tower communicated with the daily patrols over the coastline of Vietnam. Donovan tried to focus on the chatter, but Blam kept on yapping.

"But of course, *you* want to be here," Blam said with a smile.

Donovan chewed on another caramel-centered morsel. "That is correct, my friend," he began. "I come from a long —"

"A long line of military men," Blam finished. "I know all that, but don't you get sick of all the rules?"

Eyes narrowing, Donovan scoffed as he looked at his RIO in the mirror. Crumpling up the handful of foil into a small wad, Donovan threw it over his shoulder. With a small thud, the wrapper hit Blam square in the face.

"Dude!" Blam said with a laugh. The foil rolled off his chin and into his flight suit.

"Splash one!" Donovan yelled, but his joke was immediately cut short.

"Hush!" the lieutenant ordered.

A broken transmission came through the airwaves. "Marine recon unit Razor Two requesting close air support,"crackled out of Donovan's headset. Both men quickly became all business.

"That's our cue," Donovan said. He flipped on the F-4 Phantom's electrical systems. A smooth hum settled over the interior of the aircraft. Blam folded up his comic and shoved it into his hip cargo pocket.

Outside the jet, the scene around them transformed as the deck of the carrier came alive. Men in different colored vests and headgear swarmed the blacktop. They waved wild arm signals in the air like rabid third-base coaches.

High above the scene, looking down on the carrier deck from a tall tower, the commander air group spoke into a microphone. Air traffic controllers read radar screens. They made sure the skies above the carrier were cleared.

Maps of the area were hung on boards marking the enemy positions. The carrier was anchored 50 miles off the shores of Vietnam.

Below, blast shields rose out of the deck right behind the main engines of the two jets that readied for take off. In the cockpit, Blam and Candy Man sat, illuminated by the orange glow of their instruments as the catapult officer got into position on the far side of the ship.

With the engines firing full-throttle, the catapult officer put a hand to his helmet and saluted. Donovan returned the salute from the cockpit, planted his helmet firmly on the headrest, and grabbed the handhold on the right of the canopy.

Twisting his body, the catapult officer dropped to the carrier deck on one knee. He pointed forward, signaling for the launch petty officer to hit the button and fire the catapult. Flame, steam, and a loud howl from the jet's engines signaled the beginning of the mission. Donovan's F-4 Phantom shot toward the shores of Vietnam.

Once in the air, the F-4 climbed as Donovan pulled the throttle back, disengaging the afterburners. In a flash, the pilot and his RIO were over land. They streaked toward the jungles of Đong Xoài. A full moon cast an eerie hue over the tropical wilderness.

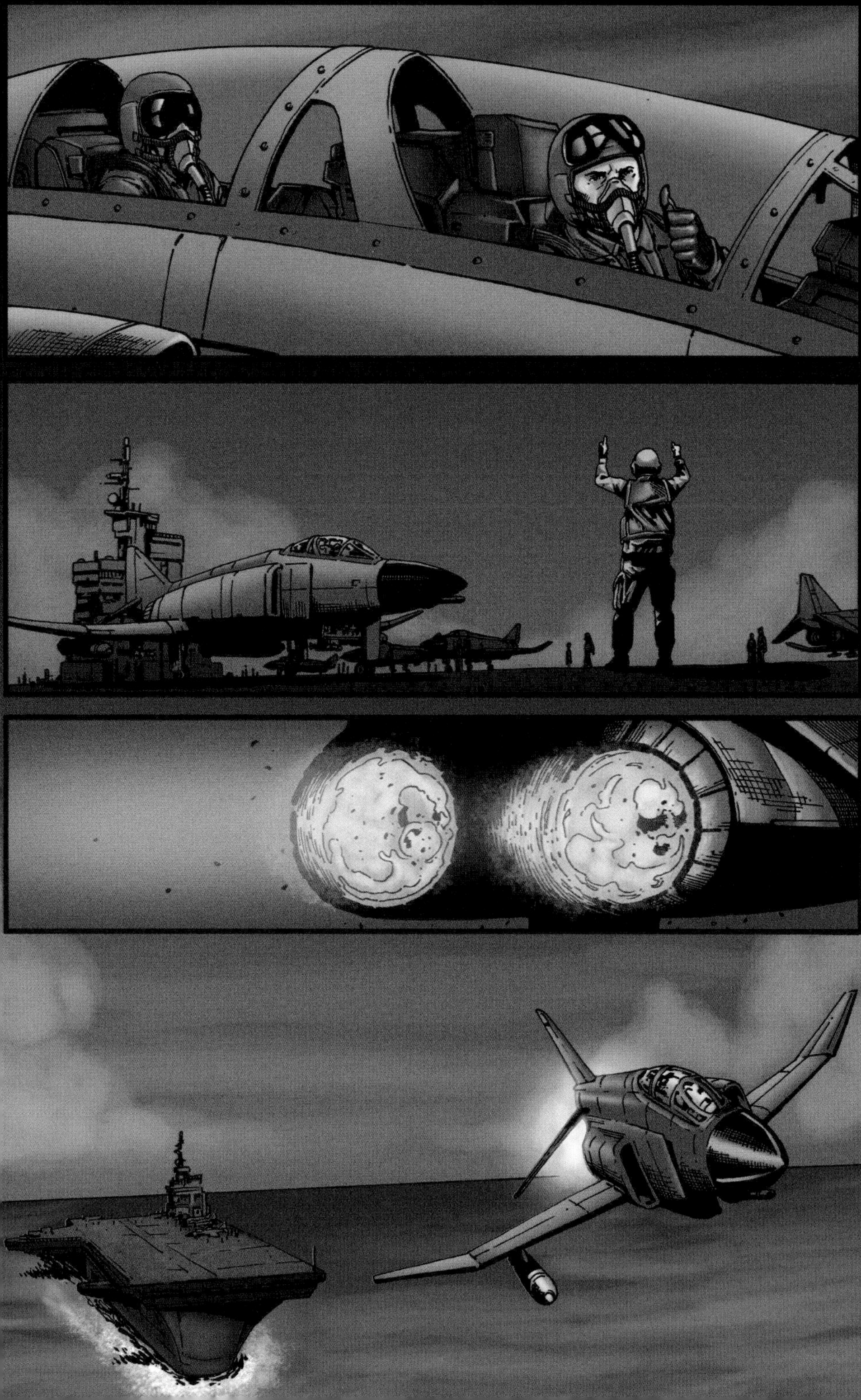

"Home Plate Zero-One, this is Iron Hand One Three Niner. We are feet dry, over," Donovan radioed.

"Roger, Iron Hand One Three Niner," the controller replied. "One more minute on that heading to the turn point, over. Coordinates Gulf, four-five-two, over."

"Roger that, Home Plate Zero One," Donovan replied.

"What have we got?" asked Blam. He swept the skies for any sign of enemy contacts from the jet's back seat.

"Looks like Marine Recon patrol, Razor Two, stumbled into a Vietcong training camp," said Donovan. "They need some help from above."

"Jarhead Marines," Blam joked. He flipped on his radar screen. "They never look where they're going. I mean come on, it's 1968, man! Don't those boys know how to read a map yet?"

"Roger that," answered Donovan. He reached down and locked a silver tab into his helmet, securing the rubber oxygen mask to his face. His eyes became narrow and confident as the 24-year-old gripped the flight stick.

The F-4 streaked through the air like lightning, and then turned sharply left, leveling its wings.

Suddenly, an energy wave appeared on Blam's scope. "I got enemy radar," he said. "It's sweeping for a target."

On the ground, hidden by a layer of camouflaged netting, a radar dish cycled back and forth. It scanned the skies for enemy contacts. Soon, it had found one.

"Activate jamming signal!" Donovan ordered.

Pressing a series of switches, Blam activated the plane's electronic countermeasures. These devices transmitted jamming signals on all frequencies, making their plane invisible to radar.

"Jamming!" he yelled as he eyed the screen intently.

"Razor Two, this is Iron Hand One Three Niner," Donovan radioed. "Request you pop yellow smoke to mark your position. We don't want Kentucky-Fried Marines for chow tonight, over."

Pops, bangs, and explosions filled his headset. "Roger that, Iron Hand!" the Marine radio operator finally answered back. "Them Vietcong are advancing north on our position. Attack against the tree line — a hundred yards northeast of our smoke!"

Whoa! Donovan thought. *That's pretty close to our friends. Those Marines must be in serious trouble.*

"Have you got it?" Donovan asked Blam as his head surveyed the tree line in front of them.

Blam smiled as a plume of yellow, wispy smoke began to rise up in the distance.

"Contact," Blam answered back. "Yellow smoke bearing two-seven-five at eleven o'clock low."

Donovan pushed the stick in that direction. "Tally ho, stepping into target," he said. "Thirty seconds."

The plane's nose dipped as Donovan pressed the stick forward. For his attack run, he lined up with the trees that whipped by him at 600 miles per hour. With a target that close, the lower he could get, the better accuracy he'd have when he released his bombs.

Beeps filled the inside of the cabin. Blam coordinated the computer system with the area the Marines had designated as the target.

"We're locked," he called out to Donovan. "Fifteen seconds to target. Arm the explosives."

Leaning in, Donovan flipped the ARM switch on his weapons panel. "Pickle's are hot," he called out.

As the target approached, they could finally see the dull glare of the fighting. Hot tracer fire from both sides filled the skies between the trees like lasers in the night. Small-arms explosions rocked the jungle floor, sending showers of mud and grime skyward.

Secretly, in that instance, Donovan was thankful that he was relatively safe in his multi-million-dollar armored jet fighter. He wasn't on the ground, slinging lead at the enemy, hip-deep in jungle mud like his father and grandfather had been decades before him.

Brought back to the fight, Donovan shook off the daydream as the beeps signaled his target was locked.

"Drop 'em and climb, Candy Man!" Blam ordered from the back seat.

Donovan pushed the button on the control stick.

Clicks echoed out underneath the plane. The safety pistons released, allowing the bombs to float away from the belly of the aircraft.

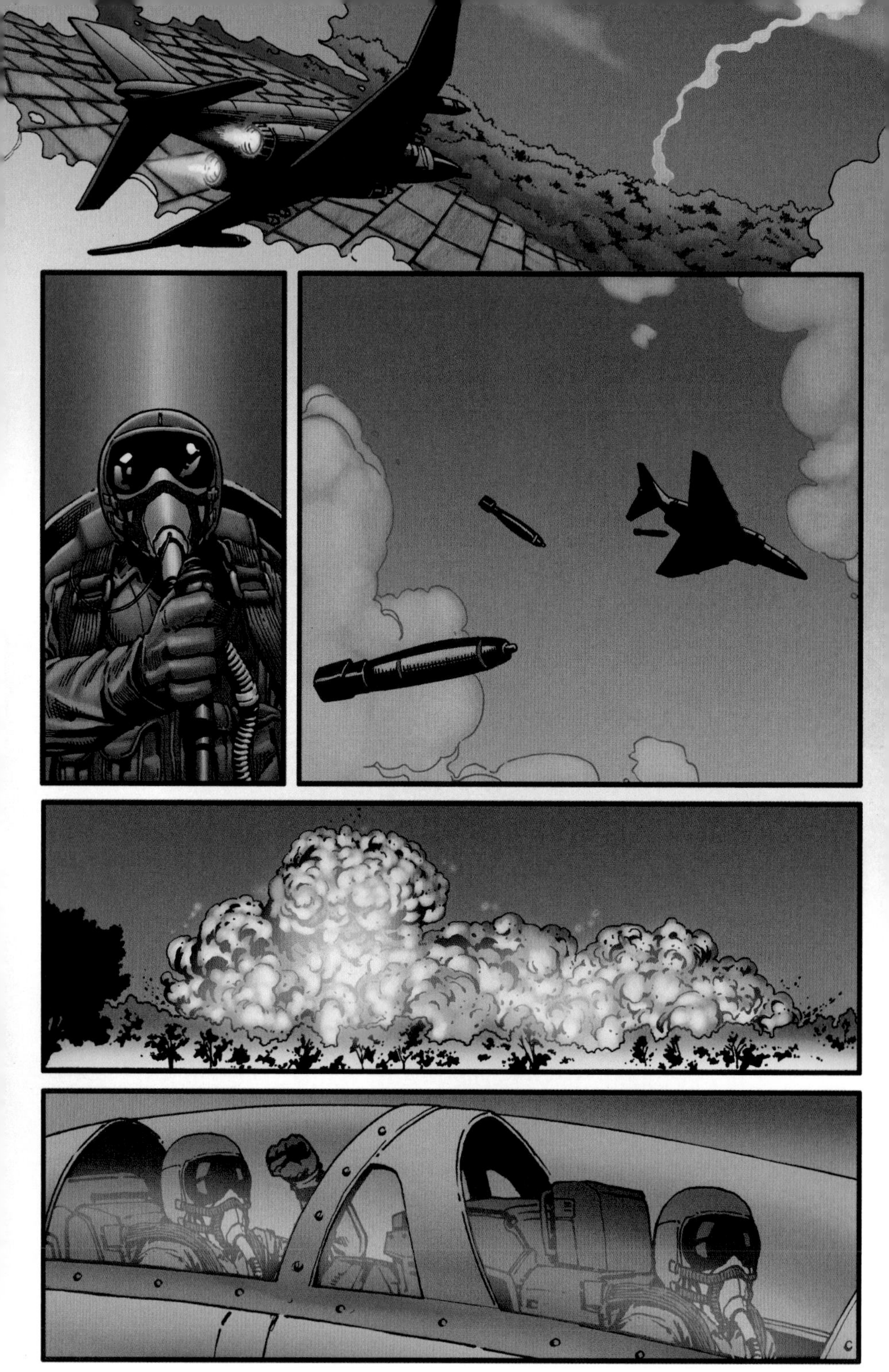

As the Mark 82 bombs fell, their tail fins splayed open, allowing a more controlled descent to the ground. Spinning lazily, the bombs dropped toward their target and, in a number of quick seconds, ignited the jungle in a rainbow of yellows and reds.

"Razor Two, Iron Hand, good strike?" Donovan radioed to the Marines on the ground.

A tense moment passed as silence filled the cockpit.

"Roger that, Iron Hand! Good shooting!" finally crackled through the static. "We all owe you a cold one when we get back to the real world!"

Smiling, Donovan nodded proudly. "Roger that," he said. "Razor Two, keep your —"

But a shrieking alarm rang out, cutting him off. On his instrumentation panel, a red MISSILE warning alarm flashed.

"Blam, what is it?!" Donovan yelled.

"An air-to-air missile!" he replied.

"Where?!" Donovan asked, his eyes scanning the horizon. But then he saw it.

A short-range, air-to-air missile lit up the night sky. It launched through the trees, did a lazy midair spin, and accelerated right for them.

"I've got it!" Donovan said. He pushed the control stick hard to the left. As the plane swept away from the deadly missile, Donovan pressed a button marked DISP on his right throttle control.

Two small discharge tubes suddenly opened above the jet's wing flaps. They sprayed a cloud of debris into the air. Donovan smiled. The thick cloud of metal filings would, hopefully, look bigger on the missile's radar than his plane did. The missile would swing toward the decoy, not the jet.

"Chaff's away!" Donovan said as he kicked in the throttle.

Behind, the missile came dead for them. Then suddenly, it turned and headed for the cloud of raining debris. Seconds later, the shock wave from the exploding missile rippled through the air.

"Yeah!" Donovan yelled, but a slight beeping from the back seat caught his attention.

Now what? he thought, but he knew exactly what those warnings meant.

"Multiple contacts! Multiple contacts!" Blam shouted from the rear seat.

"Huh?" Donovan asked.

"We've got company," his RIO replied.

F-4 PHANTOM II

SPECIFICATIONS

FIRST FLIGHT: 5-27-1958
WING SPAN: 38 feet, 11 inches
LENGTH: 62 feet, 11 inches
HEIGHT: 16 feet, 5 inches
WEIGHT: 30,328 pounds
MAX SPEED: 1,472 mph
CRUISE SPEED: 585 mph
CEILING: 60,000 feet
CREW: Two (pilot and electronic
warfare officer)

HISTORY

The F-4 Phantom II was one of
the most easily identified planes
used in the Vietnam War. This
twin-engine, all-weather fighter-
bomber was flown by three
branches of the military: U.S.
Navy, Air Force, and Marine Corps.
Pilots of the planes were called
"Phantom Phlyers." Production
of the Phantom II ended in 1979
after more than 5,000 planes had
been built. Though U.S. military no
longer uses F-4s, modern versions
continue to be used in several
other countries, including Japan,
Germany, and Iran.

FACT

The F-4 Phantom II set fifteen
world records, including ones for
absolute speed and altitude.

USS *CONSTELLATION*

SPECIFICATIONS

CLASS & TYPE: *Kitty Hawk*-class
aircraft carrier
SERVICE: 1961-2003
LENGTH: 1,088 feet
BEAM: 282 feet extreme, 130 feet
waterline
SPEED: 34 knots
PROPULSION: 8 boilers, 4 steam
turbine engines
AIRCRAFT CARRIED: 72

HISTORY

The USS *Constellation's*
service in Vietnam began with
deployment in May, 1964. On
August 4, 1964, F-4 Phantom
IIs deployed from the ship to
provide air coverage for USS
Maddox, under attack by the
North Vietnamese Navy. The
Constellation had a total of
seven wartime deployments
before the cease-fire was called
on January 23, 1973. The ship
continued to serve the U.S. Navy
until 2003, after 42 years of
service and 21 missions.

FACT

The ship was heavily damaged by
fire while under construction. Fuel
spilled on welders, starting a fire
that killed 50 people.

CHAPTER 002

THE HIT

Without hesitating, Lieutenant "Candy Man" Donovan slammed the F-4 Phantom's control stick to the right, dodging a Vympel K-13 air-to-air missile. The explosive narrowly missed the belly of his aircraft. He began to wonder what had gotten him into this situation in the first place. But there wasn't time to dwell on those thoughts now.

Donovan was in the zone. In this mental state, hyper-focused thoughts drifted, and reflex and instinct took over. The screaming enemy missile, however, brought him quickly back to reality.

Two MiG-21 aircraft had entered their airspace on radar. In seconds, the skies looked like an angry hornet's nest.

At 12,000 feet above the ground, the three planes swarmed one other, each going in different directions. As they fought for position, the jets snapped past one another like ends of wild bullwhips.

Underneath them, the earth spun. The horizon appeared and disappeared from view of the pilots time and time again.

Extreme g-forces flattened them against their seats. Candy Man strained his neck to track the enemy jets that streaked past at Mach One, over 700 miles per hour.

"Where are they!?" Donovan yelled back to Blam. He slammed the control stick to the right, causing them both to roll to the starboard side of the cockpit.

With each hard turn, Candy Man and Blam grunted. Their specialized g-suits kept blood from rushing to their brains. Still, the flyers fought to keep themselves from passing out.

"Ungh!" Donovan strained. "MiG One is moving away from us, MiG Two . . ." He looked around, attempting to see behind them.

". . . is on our right and coming fast!" he continued.

Hot lead and glowing tracers flew through the night sky. The MiG Two opened up and fired from behind, its cannon blazing. Donovan jerked the stick left and the F-4 took an astonishing turn. The second MiG roared past them, arcing wide, missing them completely.

Donovan didn't slow his pace as he powered the throttle down, dropped his flaps, and rolled the Phantom hard right. Then he thumbed the weapons selector on his control stick to GUNS.

Suddenly, the jet swung around, coming in right behind the MiG's tail. On his electronic display, an orange diamond appeared around the enemy jet. "Target locked" signals echoed in the darkness of the cockpit.

Donovan pulled the trigger. On the nose of the plane, the night illuminated as the Vulcan cannon exploded to life. It blasted molten-hot lead at the MiG.

"Come on!" Donovan grunted as he slowly adjusted his elevation. He strained to pull the bullets into the MiG's position.

After a moment, the metal slugs dug deeply into the enemy jet, causing irreparable damage to its systems. Smoke began belching from the holes in its hull. Fuel and hydraulic fluid ignited in the sky. With a resounding blast, the MiG exploded, sending a hail of flaming debris and scorched metal toward the ground below.

There was no time for celebration. The F-4 Phantom was suddenly caught in a hail of cannon fire from the first MiG. The enemy had circled back around, sweeping down from above them.

Donovan broke hard. He dove deep as both jets now streaked across the sky, low to the deck, skimming the treetops of the jungle. Pulling up and slamming the throttle into overdrive, Donovan engaged the afterburners and went completely vertical. He shot the Phantom jet up straight and hard, aiming for the moon.

"Faster, he's coming around!" screamed Blam as he looked at his scope.

Vapor trails came off the missile as the MiG launched and followed the F-4 into the night sky.

Donovan hit the DISP button again.

This time, the cloud of debris didn't work. The explosive crashed through the metal decoy cloud and kept on coming like a bloodhound with their scent. It would be on them in a matter of seconds.

Inside the cockpit, Donovan reached his hands down. He grasped the metal handle and yanked it up with all his might. Spinning left, the MiG's missile didn't even twitch. It flew straight up the Phantom's tailpipe.

The canopy flew off and away from the aircraft. The ejection seat rockets engaged, blasting both Donovan and Blam out of the plane as the missile detonated.

The U.S. fighter jet exploded in midair. Heat and flames licked at the heels of the Navy F-4 Phantom. The only remnant of the magnificent machine rained down and scattered across the jungle in a streaking pile of burning rubble.

Clicking off and falling away, the ejection seats plummeted to the earth. Their chutes popped open, catching enough air, thankfully, to deploy their main chutes. They fluttered open with a sudden pop.

In the wink on an eye, Candy Man and Blam found themselves floating earth-bound on silken cushions of air. They were headed toward certain danger . . . behind enemy lines.

MiG-21

SPECIFICATIONS

FIRST FLIGHT: 2-14-1955
WING SPAN: 23 feet, 6 inches
LENGTH: 51 feet, 9 inches
HEIGHT: 15 feet, 9 inches
WEIGHT: 18,080 pounds
MAX SPEED: 1.300 mph
RANGE: 400 miles
CEILING: 50,000 feet
CREW: One

FACT

The MiG-21 has been flown in more than 50 countries on four different continents.

HISTORY

Designed by the Mikoyan-Gurevich Design Bureau in the Soviet Union, the MiG-21 is the most produced supersonic jet aircraft in aviation history. The first MiG-21s arrived in North Vietnam from the Soviet Union by ship in April 1966. The aircraft did not have the long-range radar and missiles that the U.S. fighter planes had. However, the MiG-21 was a deadly threat in high-speed, hit-and-run attacks. This combat success led the U.S. Air Force and U.S. Navy to develop fighter training schools to improve the defense against these types of attacks.

SURFACE-TO-AIR MISSILES

HISTORY

As early as the Civil War (1861–1865), nations have searched for ways to protect themselves from aerial attacks. During WWI and WWII, this defense often came in the form of mounted, anti-aircraft guns. Soon, however, quicker and higher-flying aircraft became more difficult to defend against. In the mid-1940s, Germany developed the first guided surface-to-air missile (SAM) called the Wasserfall. Many countries, including the U.S., developed their own SAMs and by the Vietnam War, these weapons became the standard.

FACTS

– The first surface-to-air missiles of the Vietnam War were fired on July 25, 1965. The missiles struck four U.S. F-4 fighters, taking down one and damaging three.

– The SA-2 surface-to-air missile, popular during the Vietnam War, could shoot 60,000 feet into the air and travel at more than 2,500 miles per hour.

– Surface-to-air missiles are also know as ground-to-air missiles (GTAM).

CHAPTER 003

THE REALITY

Slowly, the metal top-slide on the .45 pistol glided back. The ammo magazine spring located in the handgrip released slightly, pushing a single round into the chamber. Quietly, Donovan pushed the metal slide forward, locking the bullet into the barrel, ready to be fired.

Donovan looked down at the pistol in his gloved hand and grimaced. This was a last resort. He hadn't fired a handgun since his yearly qualification time, and that was almost ten months ago.

"She's easier to operate than an airplane, fighter puke!" he remembered his USMC marksmanship instructor telling him and the other pilots. "Just point and squeeze!" They stood on the firing line squeezing triggers while aiming at paper targets across an empty field at Camp Pendleton, California.

And of course, Donovan had seen every John Wayne movie on the planet. He was pretty sure he'd be okay. Well, at close range, anyway. But these suckers were loud and would have every Vietcong patrol in a mile radius on top of him in a minute.

Slowly, Donovan looked around the darkened jungle. He tried to get his bearings and let his eyes adjust to the new environment. He was still a bit shaken. Ejecting out of a perfectly good aircraft will do that to you. But he'd gotten lucky. His descent had taken him right into a dip between two massive tree canopies, allowing him to completely miss the thick bamboo and branches on the way down. Still, he was worried about his radio officer.

Donovan stopped. He held his breath and listened for enemy patrols. *Nothing but the sounds of a typical jungle oasis,* he thought to himself, crouching next to a tree. Reaching down, he unbuckled his parachute and unzipped his g-suit, allowing them to fall to the ground. With a deep breath, Donovan moved into the trees.

About forty yards away from his landing position, Donovan saw Blam lying on the ground. He was wrapped up in his own parachute cords and not moving.

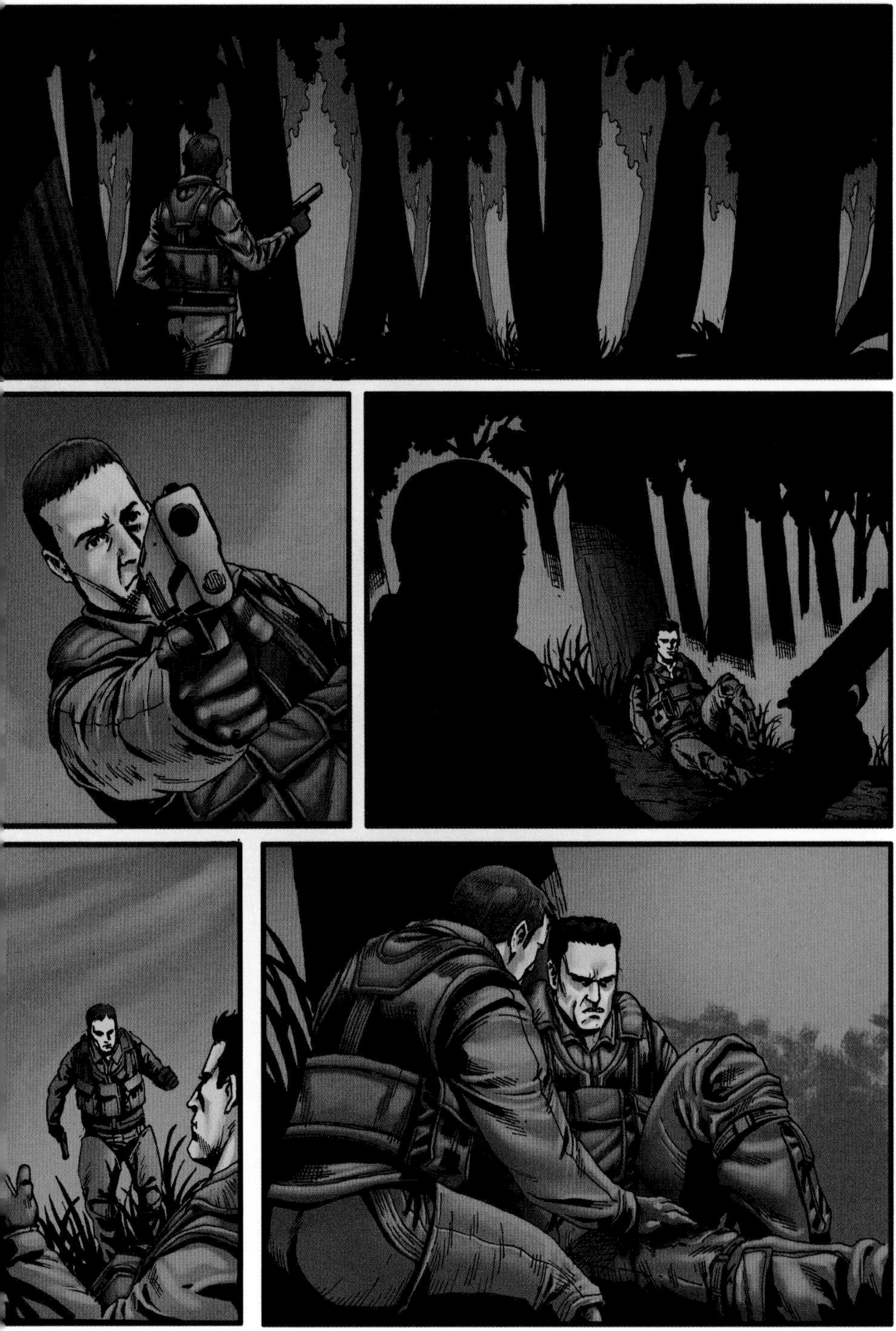

Eyes wide in fear, Donovan crouched and moved quickly. He made as little noise as possible in the dense underbrush as he moved toward his friend.

"Blam!" Donovan whispered as reached his injured side.

"Uh, man," Blam moaned weakly. "Who taught you to fly?"

Donovan smiled. He dropped to a knee and holstered his .45 caliber pistol. "Your momma," the lieutenant shot back with a grin.

Kneeling next to Blam, Donovan began unwrapping the thick nylon cord from around his friend's torso. Then he looked down and saw Blam's leg.

Splitting the fireproof fibers of the flight suit, a shard of bamboo stuck straight through the RIO's left knee. It had entered from the rear, piercing through the front of the kneecap bone.

"Oh man, this is bad," Donovan whispered.

The lieutenant pulled a small folding pocket knife from his left cargo pocket.

Blam groaned again. "Why do you think I'm still on my back?" he answered painfully.

Cutting the material, Donovan was shocked to see blood pour onto the ground. It had been pooling up inside Blam's suit since he landed. From what he could tell, the bamboo had slit an artery.

He's lost a lot of blood, Donovan thought to himself. The lieutenant tried to remember his basic battlefield lifesaving techniques. *Stop the bleeding,* he recalled and began cutting away another nylon cord. Then he looped the cord around Blam's leg and twisted it tight with a small branch.

"Blam, I'm going to tourniquet your —" started Donovan, looking over at Blam. The RIO's eyes dipped lazily and closed. Donovan reached up and slapped him hard across the cheek. Blam shook it off and woke up.

"Hey, you with me?" Donovan asked, giving Blam a good shake.

"Yeah, yeah . . . I'm back," he mumbled back as Donovan kept twisting the stick, which cut off the blood flow to the open wound.

"Thanks, Doctor Kildare," Blam said. He rested his head back against the tree. Then he unzipped his left breast pocket.

Donovan reached in and removed his short-range VHF radio. "Home Plate Zero-One, this is Iron Hand One-Three-Niner, come in, over," he said, pressing the TALK button on the handheld radio.

After what felt like a lifetime of waiting, a reply finally came. "One-Three-Niner, this is Zero One, go ahead, over," the voice said.

Donovan let a grin slip from his lips as he continued transmitting. "Iron Hand is down," he reported. I repeat, Iron Hand is down. One severely wounded and in immediate need of a medical evac, over."

"Roger that, One-Three-Niner," said the radio operator. "Check your chart."

Unzipping one of his many pockets, Donovan removed his map of the area. He unfolded it on his leg as he crouched. It was dark, but the slight moon shining through the trees allowed him enough light to read. "Roger, go," he said.

"Need you to reposition to two-niner-romeo, delta echo, 1689 2957," the radio operator relayed.

The directions confused Donovan. He traced the lines on his map with his fingers. Those map coordinates were nowhere near their position. "Confirm last?" he asked. "That's more than nine kilometers from here!"

"Confirmed," replied the RO. "Local enemy resistance is too hot for helicopter recovery in your location. We need you to relocate to rally point at those coordinates within three hours."

Donovan checked his watch.

"If you're late, we'll be gone —" the RO continued. But a rustling nearby followed by softened shouts made Donovan quickly switch off his radio.

"What is it?" Blam said weakly.

Donovan silently shushed him with a finger. He skinned his .45 pistol and cocked back the hammer.

Getting on his stomach, Donovan belly-crawled up to a log. He pulled a pair of binoculars from his right breast pocket, adjusted the focus, and took a look.

Ahead of them, about a hundred yards out, fifteen Vietcong soldiers glowed in the moonlight. Each of them carried an AK-47 and a cache of other deadly weapons. They were in a tactical wedge formation, like an arrowhead slicing through the jungle. They combed the area for something important.

Donovan grimaced.

It didn't take a rocket scientist to figure out what, or rather, *who* they were looking for.

"Vietcong. Fifteen of them," Donovan said to his injured partner. "Standard search pattern. They're looking for us."

"We need to move," Donovan continued in a whisper.

Blam shook his head in pain. "No, you do," he said. "I'll just slow you down."

"What? No!" Donovan nearly shouted. "I am not leaving you here!"

Donovan bent over to grab Blam. He started to pick him up in a fireman's carry, but the RIO slapped Donovan's hand away.

"Look," Blam said loudly, trying to get Donovan's attention. "We both know I'm not gonna make it to the pick up, especially not by five o'clock."

Donovan looked down at Blam's injury. He knew Blam was right. There was no way he'd make it another three hours, even if they weren't on the run. Two hours was the absolute amount of time you could tourniquet a limb. It had already been over forty minutes, but he didn't want to face this fact. He didn't want to admit that his best friend was going to die.

"You need to go," Blam said. "Get out of here!"

Donovan reached down one more time into a pocket and produced a tube of black camo paint. He popped it open and began spreading the black paste all over Blam's face and hands.

"Stay low in these bushes and do not move." He pushed some leaves and fallen limbs over Blam's body, covering him in the camouflage of the jungle.

Removing the RIO's pistol from his holster, Donovan placed the handgrip in Blam's palm. The RIO gripped it as tightly as he could, but the gun slipped to the ground.

Donovan tried again, but this time he placed Blam's hand in his lap and his finger against the trigger.

"I'll be back with the cavalry. I promise," said Donovan. "You just hold on, okay, just —" The lieutenant tried to choke back emotion, but his voice cracked.

Reaching out for him, Blam placed a strong hand on Donovan's forearm. "You're the best friend a guy could have, Verner," he said. "Watch your back, pal. Now go!"

Donovan rose and hesitated. He looked at Blam and smiled as his eyes began to water. He feared this would be the last time he ever saw his best friend again. Donovan nodded and with that, he was gone.

Blam sighed. He placed the back of his head against the tree, tears starting to roll down his face. He could hear the enemy now, no more than ten yards away. The gun in his hand began to quiver as the sounds of the Vietcong soldiers drew closer.

He closed his eyes, held his breath, and waited for the end to come.

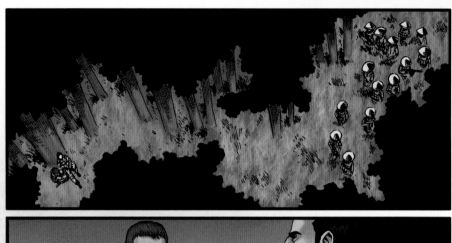

DEBRIEFING

AK-47 ASSAULT RIFLE

SPECIFICATIONS

SERVICE: 1949–present
DESIGNER: Mikhail Kalashnikov
WEIGHT: 9.5 pounds
LENGTH: 34.3 inches with fixed
wooden stock; 34.4 inches with
folding stock extended; 25.4 inches
with stock folded
BARREL: 16.3 inches
RATE OF FIRE: 600 rounds/min.
EFFECTIVE RANGE: 330 yd, full
automatic; 440 yd, semi-automatic

HISTORY

The AK-47 was first developed in
the Soviet Union. It was one of
the first true assault rifles, and it
continues to be widely used rifle
today. It remains popular because
it has a low production cost, is
easy to use, and is very durable. It
can be fired as a semi-automatic
or full-automatic rifle. In semi-
automatic mode, it fires only
once when the trigger is pulled.
In full-automatic mode, the rifle
continues to fire until the rounds
are gone or until the trigger is
released. A versatile weapon,
more AK-47s have been produced
than all other assault weapons
combined.

FACT

The AK-47 is also known as the
Kalash, a tribute to the designer.

M1911 PISTOL

SPECIFICATIONS

SERVICE: 1911–present
DESIGNER: John M. Browning
WEIGHT: 2.44 pounds
LENGTH: 8.25 inches
BARREL: 5.03 inches
HISTORY: First used by the U.S. Army on March 29, 1911, the M1911 pistol quickly became a popular weapon for all branches of the U.S. military. The single-action, semi-automatic handgun fired .45 caliber cartridges from a seven-round magazine. During WWII, the U.S. government purchased 1.9 million M1911s. They remained a vital weapon throughout the Vietnam War.

NEW WARFARE

Although handguns remained a soldier's "best friend," the U.S. military's reliance on short-range weapons and close quarters combat (CQC) decreased after WWII. Pistols and hand grenades helped troops secure combat zones and protect themselves in enemy-occupied areas. During Vietnam, the military often relied on aerial bombers and precision weapons to complete these types of tasks.

CHAPTER 004
THE SECRET

Cautiously, Donovan cut through the jungle at a full sprint. He tried not to make any noise as he traveled the overgrown jungle at top speed. There were no roads, no trails, and no landmarks to indicate he was moving in the right direction.

Several times Donovan stopped and checked his compass against his map. He needed to make sure he was heading toward the pick-up point. It was a good thing he'd paid attention in land navigation class, or he'd be in a world of hurt right about now. He didn't even have the stars to guide him, thanks to the canopy of trees shielding the skies.

Donovan couldn't believe what he had done to Blam, and it was eating at him. One of the codes of being a soldier is "leave no man behind." Still, he knew that neither of them would have made it out of that situation alive if he had stayed.

Their only chance for survival was if Donovan got to the evac point in time. Then he could call in Blam's position for pick up. That way, Blam might just make it.

Might, Donovan thought. *Who am I kidding?!*

He stopped running for a moment, trying to catch his breath. For more than forty minutes, he'd been at full sprint, putting as much distance between himself and the crash site as possible. Through fear and exhaustion, doubt started creeping into his mind. The emotions building up inside of him suddenly exploded in a burst of his hot tears.

What had he done? He'd left his best friend, scared and all alone. And for what? To save his own hide?

Donovan thought of Blam sitting against that tree, bleeding, left to suffer in the jungle. He'd surely die of blood loss or at the hands of the enemy.

There's no way he'll be able to hang on until the morning, Donovan told himself. *I should have stayed! I should have fought!* The lieutenant slammed his fist against his thigh with anger.

Feeling dizzy, Donovan reached out toward a tree for balance, but he missed completely. Stumbling, Donovan felt the ground below him give way. A complex structure of tree limbs and hemp rope snapped and fell apart beneath him. They had been camouflaged by leaves and twigs.

Luckily, Donovan shifted his weight. He moved just in time as a man-sized pit open up beneath him. Crawling to its edge, he looked down and cringed.

A hole about ten-feet deep, five-feet across had been revealed. At the bottom of the hole, thick bamboo poles faced upward, their tips sharpened into deadly points. Each pole had been smeared with dried animal feces to promote infection. This was a punji stick trap.

Donovan had heard Marines on the carrier talk about these booby-traps. He never believed they were actually real. Punji sticks were usually used by the Vietcong in preparation for an ambush, with the enemy soldiers lying in wait to pop out and surprise the Marines. The plan was that U.S. soldiers would dive for cover and impale themselves on the poisoned bamboo spears.

The sight of the trap made Donovan's stomach turn. *How could anyone do such a horrible thing to another human being?* he wondered. Then the lieutenant looked at the gun in his own hand. *Was one weapon more horrible than the other?*

A sharp noise caught Donovan's attention. In a flash, he spun, raised his weapon in the air, and took aim. Eyes wide, the lieutenant hesitated to pull the trigger.

A Vietnamese girl, about six years old and her fifteen-year-old brother stood frozen in front of him. Fear washed over them. They didn't dare move.

"You American?" the boy asked in broken English.

Slowly, Donovan raised his empty hand in the air. He lowered his pistol and nodded.

"We saw plane crash," the boy said. "That you?"

Donovan nodded again as he measured up the boy. He was about five-feet, four-inches tall and dressed in a blue shirt with black cotton pants. Both of the children's feet were clothed in leather slippers, which appeared to be made from scraps of water buffalo hide.

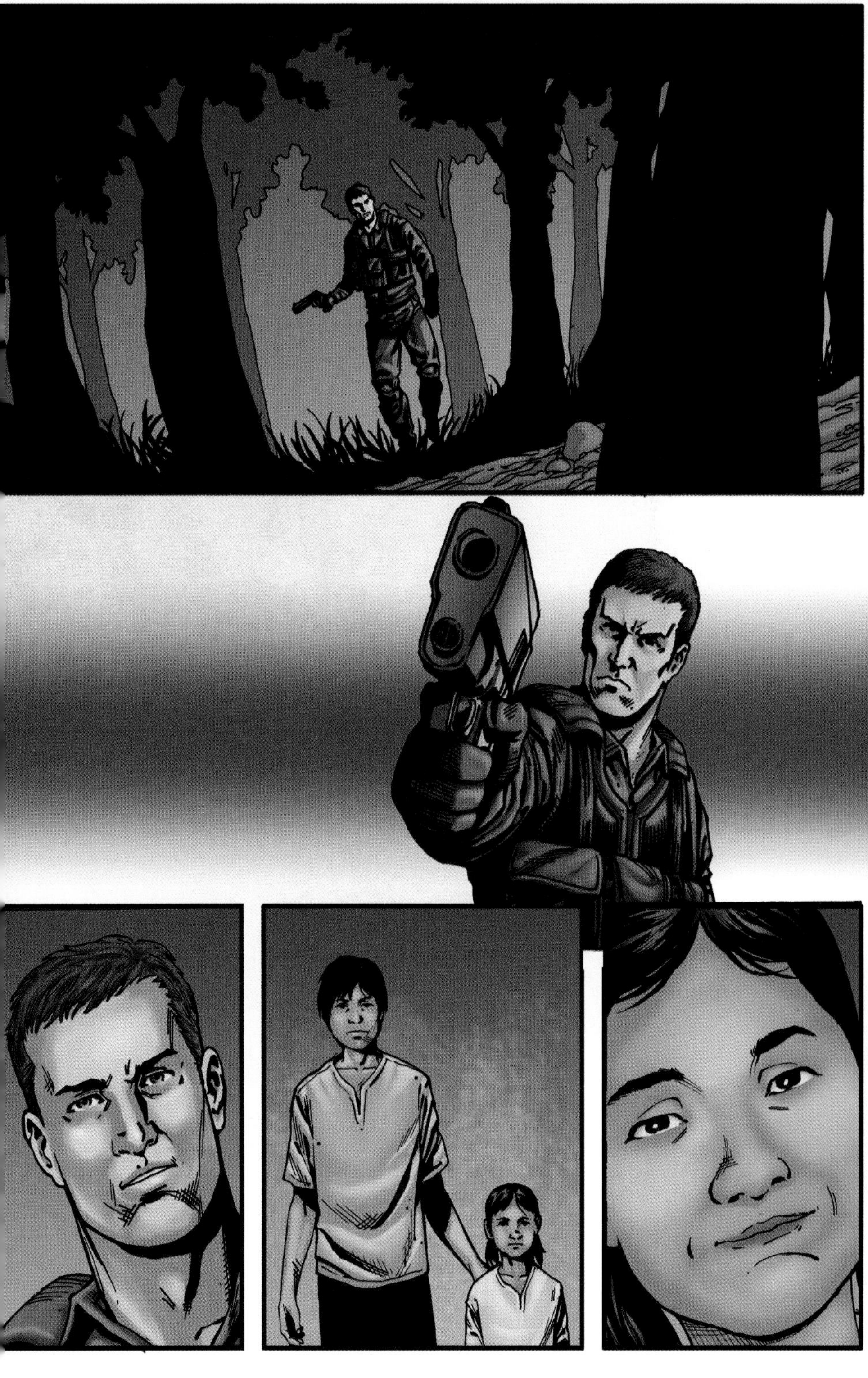

"Come with us!" the teenage boy said. He turned and pointed behind him. "Village not far. Patrols many here. We hide you!"

Lieutenant Donovan was weary of the goodwill. He wasn't getting much of that these days, and he wasn't sure why these kids would want to help him.

The little girl walked over and placed a small hand on his forearm. She smiled. "We help," she squeaked out of her small face.

Donovan stood, holsetering his weapon, and grabbed the girl's hand. She and her brother led him deeper into the jungle.

*   *   *

A short time later, Donovan walked into what looked like the world that time forget. Small grass huts, called hooches, made of bamboo frames and mud-covered turf lined the small dirt road. Some of the huts had small wooden fences surrounding the sides or backs of the homes. Livestock, such as pigs and chickens, roamed throughout most of the tiny village.

Though morning was just about to crack over the horizon, Donovan could tell the village was still asleep. Only a few open windows flickered with candlelight. High above, banana trees rose a hundred feet into the air, allowing protection from the tropical sun and plentiful harvest come picking time.

The poor lifestyle amazed Donovan. He thought there was something peaceful about it all, like the way a Midwest farm must have been at the turn of the century. The land was untamed. The Vietnamese people were hoping to conquer it and better their society and culture. Donovan respected those goals. He hoped to craft his own plot of land when he finally returned home.

The children led Donovan across the dirt road and into their home. The lieutenant ducked through the curtain-covered doorway.

The home was modest and small. Pieces of matting covered the dirt floors. Furniture was sparse, not even a couch. A simple set of handmade wooden chairs surrounded a small table, which had been crafted out of pieces of bamboo.

Donovan didn't have a second to rest. The childrens' mother came charging out of her bedroom as soon as the lieutenant entered. She took one look at the U.S. soldier and began yelling at the children.

The mother pointed at Donovan and screamed in Vietnamese at the young boy. He waved his hands in the air, pleading with her and trying to calm her down.

"He needs our help!" he said in his native language, but his mother didn't seem to care.

"No," she replied. "No! He does not stay here! You make him go! All he'll bring is death to this family!"

"If we don't help him," the boy replied, "then we're no better than the soldiers that burn our homes!"

Donovan slumped down on the bench, exhausted. Even as the mother screamed, he took a moment to relax and let the rest of the world fade away.

Donovan looked at his watch and frowned. The face had cracked somewhere along the line. But the antique watch was keeping perfect time. The second hand ticked from one hash mark to the next.

Great, he thought, *I can't even keep grandpa's watch safe, let alone myself.*

Amazed, Donovan did a double-take and checked the time again. It was now only sixty minutes before his pick up. Precious time was slipping away.

Then Donovan thought about Blam. Had it really already been two hours? Was he still alive? Would they be able to get to him even if the U.S. soldiers picked him up on time? His thoughts turned to fear again. Fear for Blam. Fear for himself.

Donovan wondered if this was how his uncle felt during World War II. He had been trapped behind enemy lines in a small farmhouse in Germany on D-Day in 1944. Though his uncle didn't talk about the Great War much, he had taken Lester aside shortly before leaving for Vietnam.

His uncle looked young Donovan dead in the eyes, and said, "Fear is only an emotion, Verner. If you can control your fear, you can make it through anything. It took me a while to figure that out in France. You, however, should never forget it."

Now, Verner Donovan understood those words better than ever, especially as he studied the family that'd taken him in.

The boy was afraid of sitting by and doing nothing. If he didn't help the Americans fight this war, then he'd be no better than their enemy. The mother was obviously afraid of getting caught with an American fugitive. She knew the Vietcong would punish her swiftly.

And the little girl? Donovan looked over at her again. She stood in the corner of the small room staring at him. He tried to smile at her, but she was suddenly afraid of him. Obviously, what her mother was saying to them in Vietnamese was beginning to sink in. The black camo paint streaking his face probably didn't help either.

Slowly, Donovan reached into his pocket. He pulled out a chocolate bar in a brown and silver wrapper. As he began to peel the aluminum foil back to reveal the soft, sweet bar underneath, the young girl's eyes went wide.

Donovan reached out and offered it to her. Slowly, she walked across the room and took it from him. The adult-sized candy bar dwarfed her little hands.

The chocolate had started to melt in the heat of the humid jungle. With every bite, candy smeared across the girl's face and cheeks.

The child plopped down next to Donovan, no longer afraid. He pulled out his compass and map to double-check his coordinates. Donovan saw the clearing for pick-up was only about half a mile north from his current location. He decided to get moving.

"Look, kids, I appreciate what you did and are trying to do," Donovan said, folding his map. "But I gotta be somewhere in —"

The sound of an engine outside suddenly caught everyone's attention. Even the hysterical mother became suddenly silent. Lunging at him, the mother grabbed Donovan by the back of the collar and shoved him into her room. Then she shielded the entryway with a curtain as two Vietcong soldiers stormed into the home, armed with AK-47s.

As the men glanced around the room, the mother quickly gathered up her children. She pushed them behind her for safety.

On the other side of the curtain, Donovan quietly crouched. He removed his pistol from his holster and cocked back the hammer.

The taller Vietcong soldier pushed past the mother and looked around the room. He explained to her that they were looking for American soldiers involved in a plane crash about four miles away. "Have you seen them?" he shouted. "They came this way."

The mother shook her head as the shorter soldier flipped over the table. "Tell us!" he demanded.

"No one is here!" she yelled back as the soldiers began tearing apart the room, looking for the American.

Then the short soldier glanced down at the little girl. The chocolate smeared across her face made the angry man start to laugh. "Ha! They're so poor, they're eating mud now!" he exclaimed.

The tall soldier turned to see for himself. Crouching, he held the little girl's face. With a finger he swiped at the mud and smelled it. Looking down, he saw the candy bar still clutched in the girl's small hand.

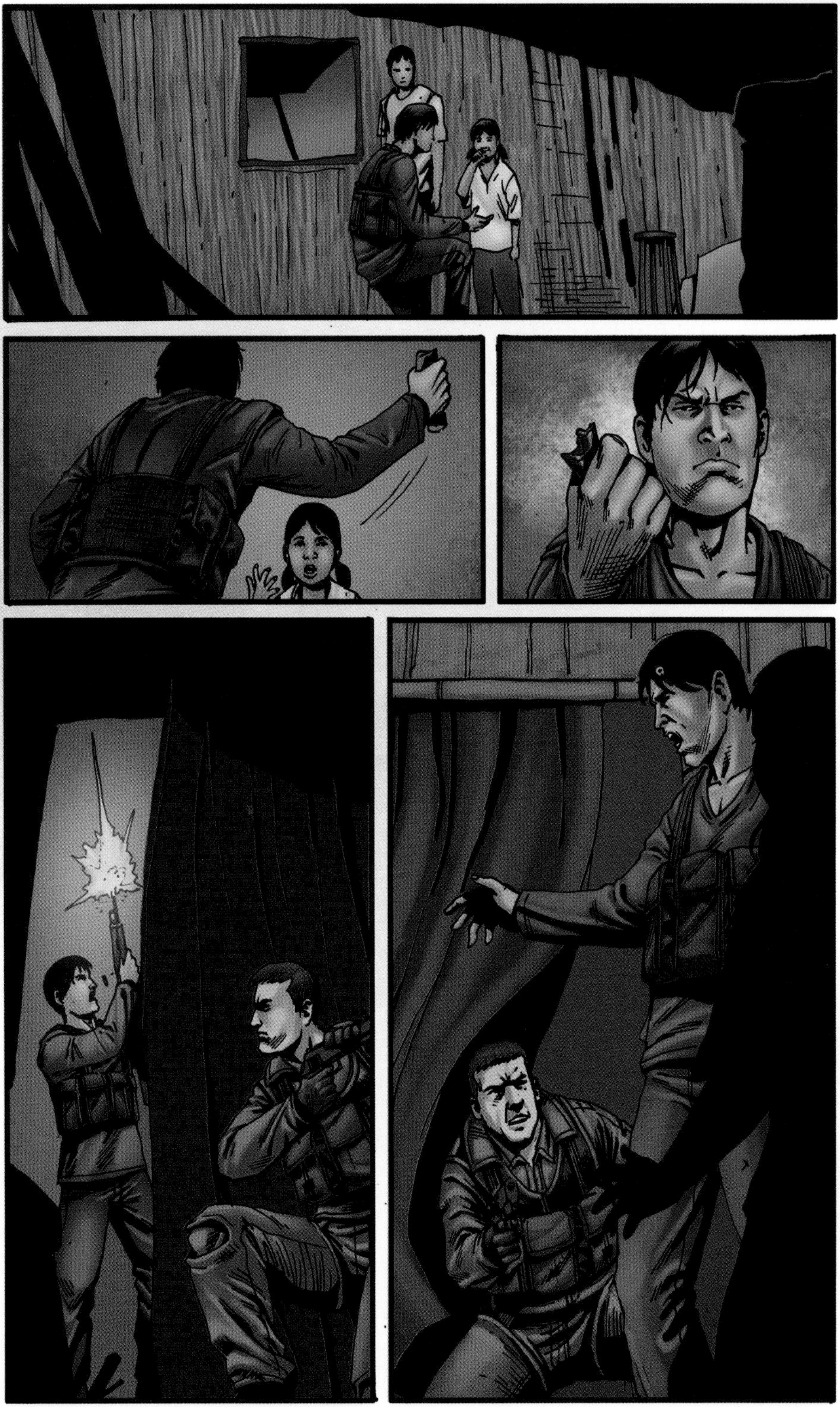

The soldier rose and glared at the mother. Without warning, the man lashed out. He struck the mother on the face. "Where are they?!" he shouted.

The mother buckled to the floor, clutching her head. The little girl ran to the corner of the room, collapsed, and began to cry. Knowing he needed to do something to protect his family, the teenager rushed the soldiers, but a boot to the chest sent the boy reeling to the dirt floor.

Then the shorter soldier racked the heavy metal action on his weapon. He chambered a round and raised his rifle in the air, about to open fire on the mother.

Suddenly, the wall to the hooch exploded open as Donovan burst in from the other room. The lieutenant tackled the short soldier to the ground.

The other Vietcong soldier turned to open fire, but the trigger jammed. His weapon was on safe.

This brief moment was all the time Donovan needed. He spun and got off two quick shots. The tall soldier fell over the legs of the table and rolled onto the dirt. He wouldn't be getting up.

The short soldier lashed out. He hit Donovan in the face with the butt of his rifle, causing the lieutenant to roll off of his Vietcong enemy. Kneeling, the soldier spun his weapon around and took aim at Donovan. As the soldier was about to fire, the young man leaped to his feet, jumping in between Donovan and the soldier.

A single shot discharged from the enemy's weapon. On the far side of the room, the teenage boy collapsed to the ground. Blood gushed from his chest.

Donovan turned to fire, but his aim was off. He missed the soldier, but the shot was enough to scare the man off. The Vietcong hastily exited the hooch and drove off in his truck.

Meanwhile, the mother rushed to her son's side. She cradled him in her arms as precious life seeped from his chest.

Donovan tried to help, to apply some life-saving techniques. The mother wouldn't let Donovan near him. She just held the lifeless body of her son close to her. She yelled at him in Vietnamese and pointed to the door hysterically.

"Go!" the mother screamed.

Donovan looked over at the little girl.

She was unharmed, but terrified. She sat huddled under the broken table, crying.

"I . . . I'm sorry," pleaded Donovan. "I . . ." But there were no words he could say. There was nothing he could do to fix these wounds.

The lieutenant picked up his gun and ran into the morning light.

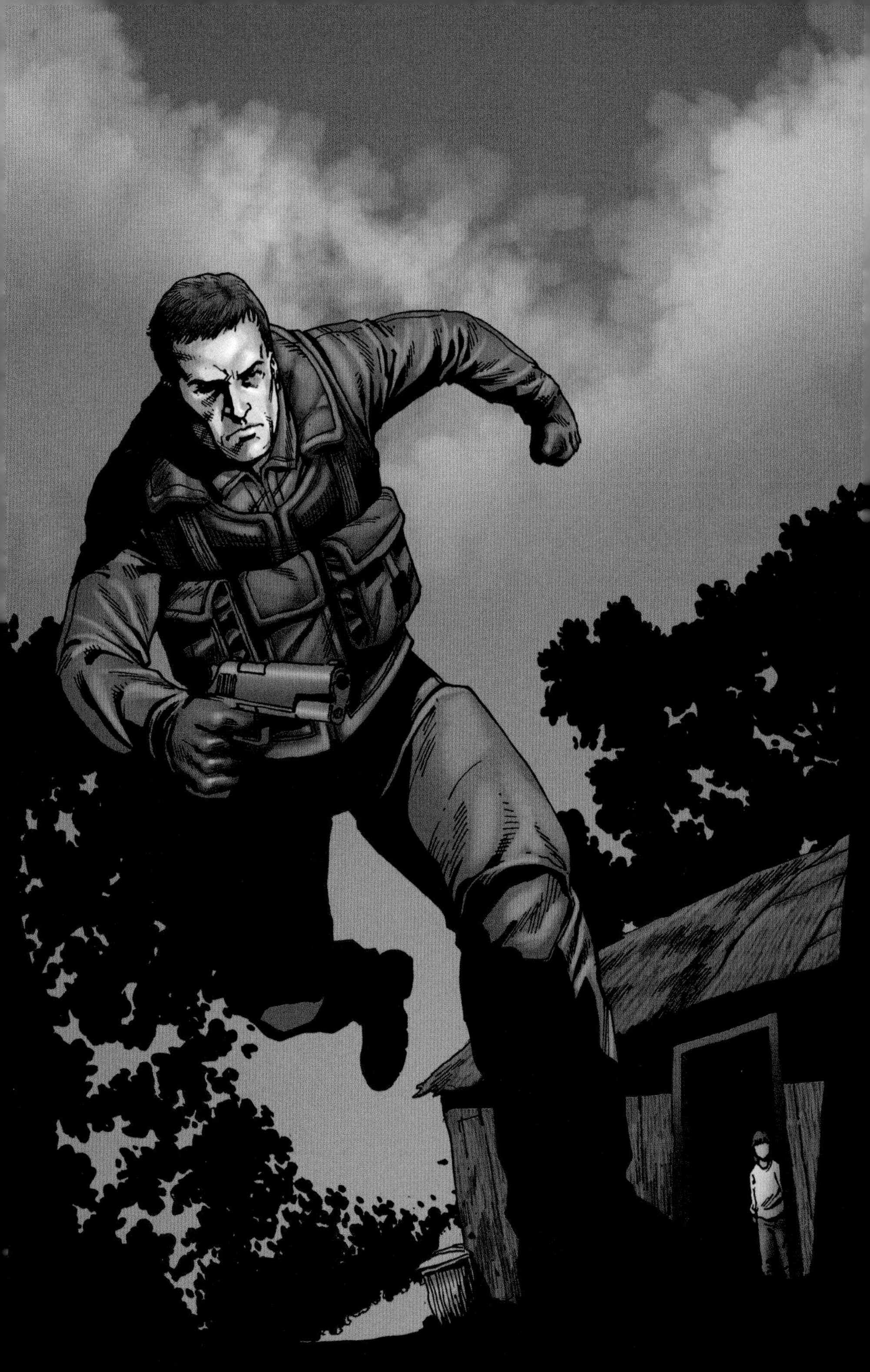

DEBRIEFING

VIETCONG SOLDIERS

BACKGROUND

The Vietcong were people in South Vietnam who supported communism. They fought with the North Vietnam military to reunite the two countries into one. These soldiers were trained and supported by North Vietnam's government. Most of the Vietcong were young teens. Many believed in the communist cause. Others had been shamed into joining. Women also took up the Vietcong cause and trained and fought with the men.

COMBAT STYLE

The Vietcong were guerrillas. Guerrillas are not part of a regular army. They often use surprise attacks against their enemies. American soldiers were trained to fight on an open battlefield with tanks, artillery, and warplanes. The Vietcong lacked this expensive equipment. Instead, they surprised their enemies with mortar and gun attacks. They also planted mines along the jungle trails. When the Americans searched through the jungles, many were killed by mines. This style of war was not as familiar to American soldiers and led to high casualties.

LIFE IN VIETNAM

CIVILIANS

The Vietcong often lived with the residents of small villages. Some South Vietnamese citizens supported the Vietcong. They helped the guerrillas. Villagers sometimes hid weapons for the Vietcong, and they often refused to answer questions about the guerrillas. Other civilians did not agree with the Vietcong cause, but they helped because they were afraid they would be killed if they did not show their support. Because the Vietcong lived so closely with the civilians, U.S. soldiers could often not tell who were friends and who were enemies.

STATISTICS

The Vietnam War claimed millions of victims. Exact casualty figures are unavailable, but below are official estimates:

GROUP	TOTAL DEATHS
U.S. Military	58,000
S. Vietnam Military	266,000
N. Vietnam Military	849,000
Vietcong	251,000
Civilians	2,000,000

CHAPTER 005
THE EFFECTS

Donovan ran as fast as he could, but he couldn't escape his problems. All around him, the lieutenant heard shouts and loud bangs. The sounds came again, but this time, they had many, many friends. Finally, he figured it out. He was hearing the shouts of Vietcong soldiers coming up behind him, firing in his direction.

Breaking from the cover of the bushes, Donovan ran into an open field. He scanned the skies, radio to his ear. "The LZ is hot! I repeat, the LZ is hot!" he yelled as bullets whizzed by. "Where the heck are you guys?!"

Above him, the whumping of large metal blades chopped through the air. A Marine UH-1 helicopter ripped over the trees and hovered on his position.

"Keep your pants on, Iron Hand One-Three-Niner!" echoed over his radio. Donovan looked up and saw the chopper crew chief throw a rescue hoist out of the bird.

As it hit the ground, Donovan climbed into the harness and gave a thumbs-up to the chief.

Like a worm on a hook, Donovan rose through the air attached to the cable. On the ground, coming out of cover of the trees, twenty Vietcong soldiers opened fire on the chopper. The helicopter dipped and swayed, trying to evade the bullets.

Several rounds ricocheted off its hull and pierced the canopy. One round pierced the bottom window, shattering the lower cockpit. The pilot ducked. "Come on, Marine, get some!" he shouted to the gunner.

In the doorway, the sergeant manning the M-60 machine gun ratcheted the charging handle. He squeezed the trigger. The weapon sprang to life. Brass casings flew out of the ejection port and rained to the ground below. The enemy soldiers scattered and ran, diving for cover.

Still dangling from the cable, Donovan shielded himself from the enemy fire. Scalding-hot friendly shell casings rained down on him in buckets. Looking up, he could see how far he had to go. But from this height, going down was an even worse option.

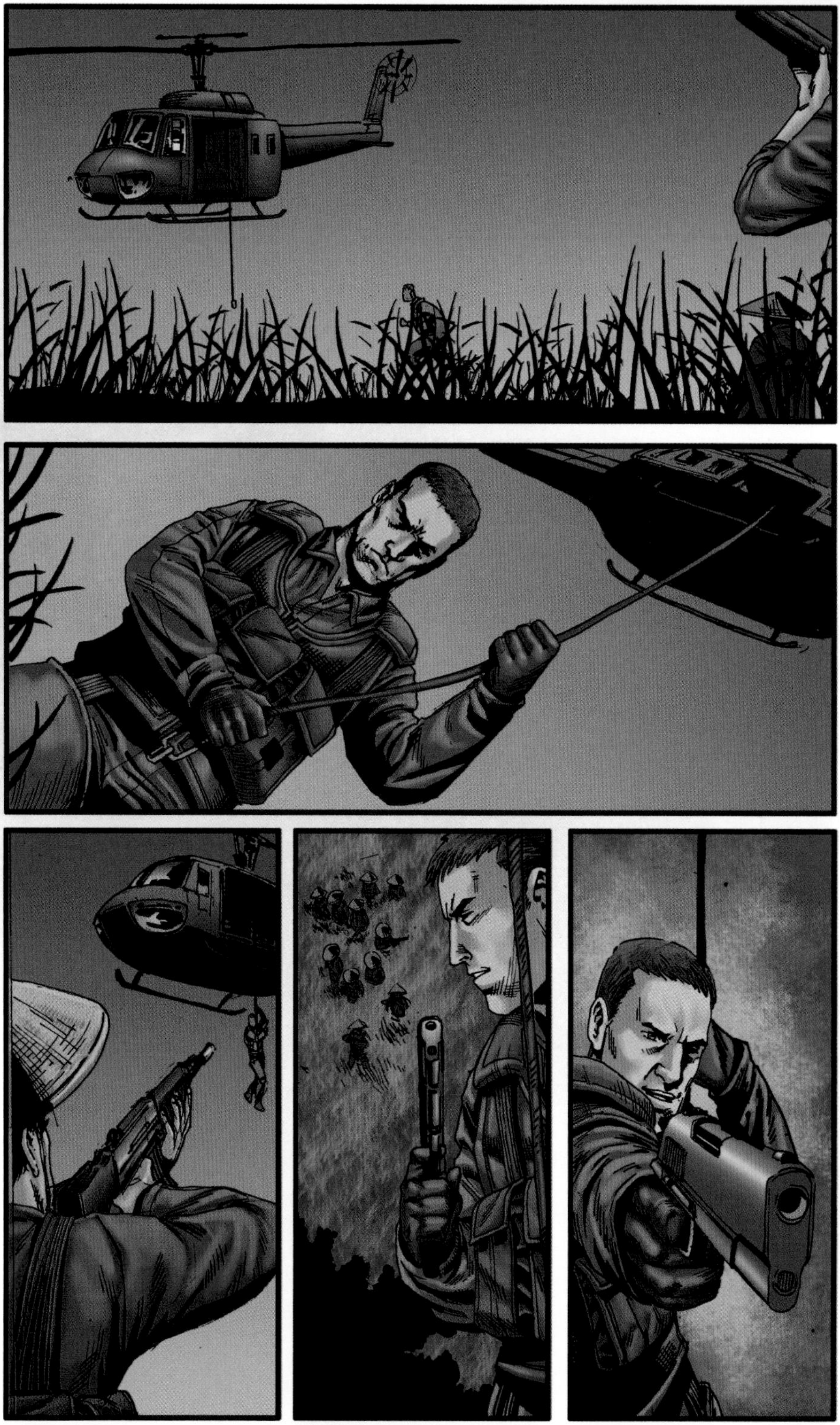

And that's when Donovan saw him . . .

The short soldier, who had killed the young teen, was breaking cover of the trees. He kneeled on a dirt road and stuffed a rocket-propelled grenade into a shoulder-mounted firing tube.

Donovan tried yelling a warning to the gunner, but he wasn't close enough to the doorway. The sergeant couldn't hear him either. The sounds of the battle were too loud.

As Donovan hung in the air, slowly rising toward the chopper, he skinned his .45 pistol. The lieutenant took aim at the Vietcong soldier below. The man had lifted the heavy RPG onto his right shoulder and flipped up the aiming site.

Donovan brought the gun up, sweat rolling down his face, and aimed. While lining up the sights, the words of his Marine marksmanship instructor echoed in his head. "Just point and squeeze!" they repeated.

Then Donovan squeezed the trigger. A single brass casing flipped end over end out of the weapon.

On the ground, the short soldier's shoulder jerked to the right. He tripped backward, pulling the trigger on the RPG as he fell.

Donovan's eyes went wide. The grenade flew right at them, a trail of bright white smoke flooding the air. Thankfully, the deadly explosive careened right, missing the chopper and flying by the front of the aircraft.

Finally, after what seemed like an eternity, a sergeant grabbed Donovan by the scruff of the neck and yanked the lieutenant into the cabin. "We've got him!" he shouted to the pilot. "Go, go, go!"

The gunner finished his job. Then he stowed the weapon and slammed the cabin door shut. The chopper banked left, picking up speed.

Streaking away over the thick jungles of Vietnam, Donovan watched through the door window. The rising sun cast an eerie orange-blue hue over the tropical wilderness.

This would be a sunrise he would never forget.

*   *   *

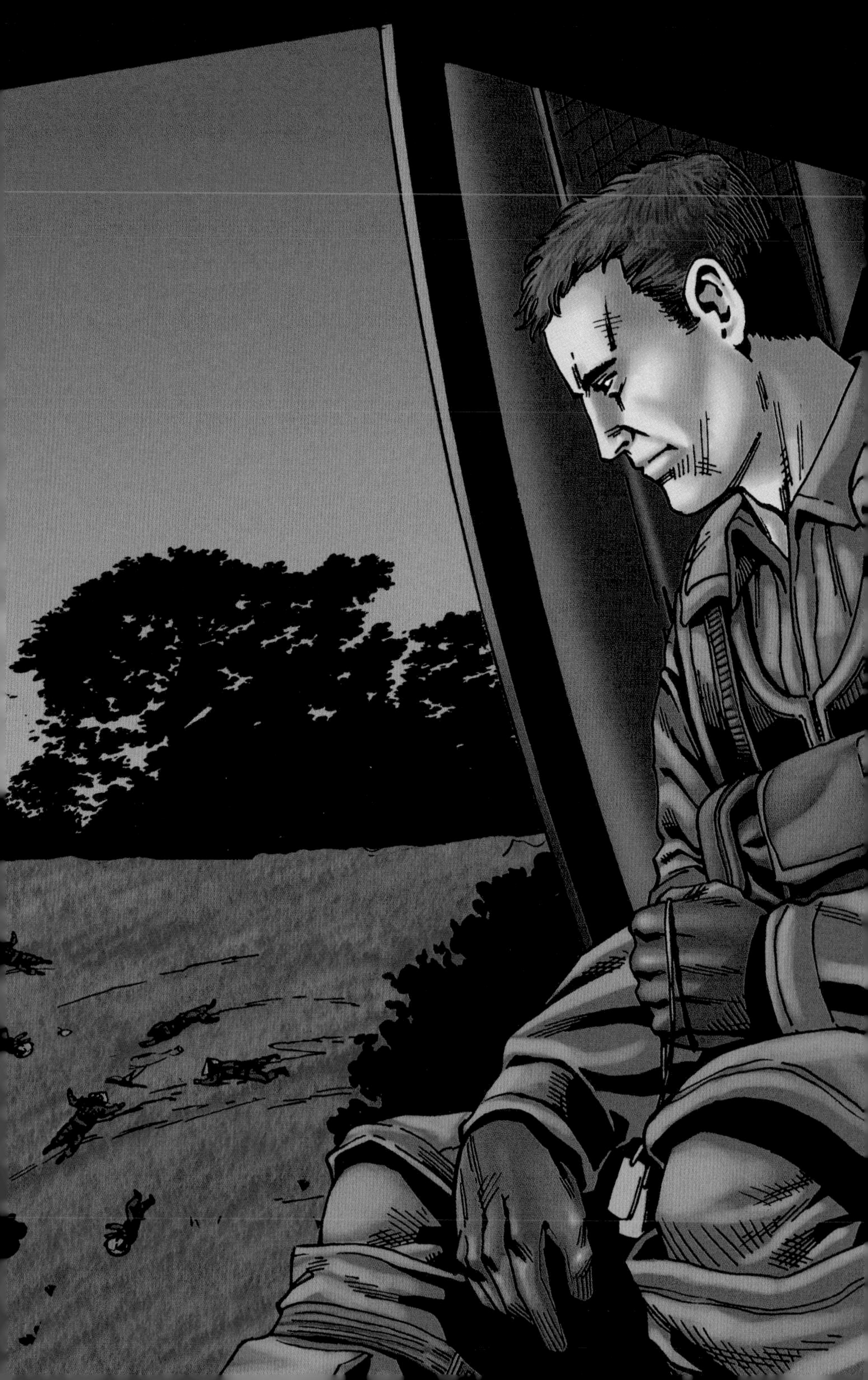

A few weeks later, Verner "Candy Man" Donovan sat on the edge of a hospital ward bed. White cotton sheets felt alien to him now. Running his hands over the smooth linen, he couldn't help but think of that Vietnamese mother having to clean up the mess he'd made.

Her dirt floors covered with rattan matting. The rattan matting now covered with her son's blood.

"How are you, Donovan?" said a voice. Entering through the main hatch was the ship's skipper, Captain Harold Neef.

Donovan stood. "Ready to fight, sir," he said.

The captain smiled. "Why don't you take some downtime, son," he said. "Fall out of rotation for a while."

"No, sir," Donovan interrupted. "With all due respect, I'd like to be on the detail that goes in for Blam, sir."

Steely-eyed, he looked Donovan in the face. "Blam's dead, son," the captain said.

"The Vietcong, did they —?" Donovan started.

The captain slowly shook his head.

"No, the enemy never found him," said the captain. "You hid him well, son. Corpsman with the unit thinks he just fell asleep from the blood loss and didn't wake up, if that's any consolation."

Donovan nodded. "It's something, sir."

The lieutenant looked up at the captain. "He was my RIO, my friend. I —" Donovan stopped. He choked back tears. His gaze wavered as his eyes shifted to the floor.

"I was responsible for him," he said. "I failed him."

"You didn't fail anyone, Donovan," the captain said. "Look at me, son. You did everything you could. Blam knew it would mean both your lives if you tried to save him. There was no way he would let you do that. Understand me?"

Donovan nodded again. "Sir?" he asked. "Is it all worth it? What we do?"

Quietly, the captain turned and sat down next to him on the bed. He thought about Donovan's question. Finally, he sucked in a breath and looked up at the lieutenant.

"There's a bigger picture out there, son," the captain responded. "Bigger than you, me, and even bigger than this ship. It's that bigger picture that matters because when liberty is taken away from somebody by force, it can only be restored by force."

Donovan nodded.

The captain continued. "But when it's given up voluntarily, that's when it can never be recovered," he said. "Pilots, and even RIOs, volunteer for this duty. We know the risk. But we face that risk every day knowing our sacrifices make a difference in the bigger picture."

Donovan was touched by the captain's words, but it didn't stop the hurt of knowing his best friend's life was over. The captain rose and headed toward the main hatch of the carrier.

"Blam's still gone, sir," Donovan said quietly.

The captain stopped in the hatchway and smiled. "Son," he said without pause, "as long as you remember the man, he'll never truly be gone."

Donovan saluted his skip. "Aye aye, sir," he said.

M-60 MACHINE GUN

STATISTICS

SERVICE: 1957-present
WEIGHT: 23.15 pounds
LENGTH: 43.5 inches
BARREL: 22 inches
FIRE RATE: 600 rounds/min
RANGE: 1,200 yards
WARS: Vietnam War
Cambodian Civil War
Gulf War
War in Afghanistan
Iraq War

HISTORY

Developed in the 1940s to replace aging automatic rifles, the M-60 quickly became a popular weapon of the U.S. military. Officially adopted by the Army in 1957, this gas-operated, belt-fed, automatic machine gun could fire nearly 600 rounds per minute. Its furious rate of fire and heavy size often made the M-60 difficult to operate. However, in the hands of a trained, three-man crew, the weapon provided effective cover fire in many situations. Even today, the U.S. Army relies on the M-60 for its military campaigns.

FACT

During the Vietnam War, the M60 became known as "The Pig" because of its large size.

UH-1 HELICOPTER

SPECIFICATIONS

FIRST FLIGHT: 10-22-1956
ROTOR DIAMETER: 48 feet
LENGTH: 57.3 feet
HEIGHT: 14.9 feet
MAX SPEED: 139.15 mph
RANGE: 197.8 miles
CEILING: 14,200 feet
HISTORY: In the early 1950s, the U.S. Army selected the UH-1 as their medical evacuation helicopter. The twin-piloted, twin-engine vehicle quickly took on a variety of tasks during Vietnam, including transportation and air assaults. More than 7,000 UH-1s served in the conflict, but more than half were destroyed in battle.

U.S. WITHDRAWL

After more than ten years of conflict and increasing political pressure, President Nixon began withdrawing U.S. troops from Vietnam in 1972. On January 27, 1973, the United States and North and South Vietnam signed a cease-fire agreement known as the Paris Peace Accords. However, as the final U.S. troops left Vietnam, the North attacked the South. They surrendered to communist rule, becoming the Socialist Republic of Vietnam.

EXTRAS

THE DONOVAN FAMILY

Like many real-life soldiers, the Donovan family has a history of military service. Trace their courage, tradition, and loyalty through the ages, and read other stories of these American heroes.

Renee Woodsworth
1925-1988

Michael Donovan
1926-1979

Military Rank: PFC
World War II
featured in *A Time for War*

Robert Donovan
1907-1956

Richard Lemke
1933-2001

Lillian Garvey
1905-1941

Mary Ann Donovan
1929-1988

Marcy Jacobson
1918-1941

Everett Donovan
1932-1951

Military Rank: CAPT
Korean War
featured in *Blood Brotherhood*

John Donovan
1946-2010

Harriet Winslow
1949-present

Tamara Donovan
1948-1965

Steven Donovan
1952-present

Terry Donovan
1971-present

Elizabeth Jackson
1973-present

Robert Donovan
1976-present

Katherine Donovan
1980-present

Michael Lemke
1954-present

Jacqueline Kriesel
1954-present

Donald Lemke
1978-present

Amy Jordan
1984-present

Verner Donovan
1951-present

Military Rank: LT
War in Vietnam
featured in *Fighting Phantoms*

Jenny Dahl
1953-2004

Lester Donovan
1972-present

Military Rank: LDCR
War in Afghanistan
featured in *Control Under Fire*

EXTRAS

ABOUT THE AUTHOR

M. ZACHARY SHERMAN is a veteran of the United States Marine Corps. He has written comics for Marvel, Radical, Image, and Dark Horse. His recent work includes *America's Army: The Graphic Novel*, *Earp: Saint for Sinners*, and the second book in the SOCOM: SEAL Team Seven trilogy.

AUTHOR Q&A

Q: Any relation to the Civil War Union General William Tecumseh Sherman?

A: Yes, indeed! I was one of the only members of my family lineage to not have some kind of active duty military participation – until I joined the U.S. Marines at age 28.

Q: Why did you decide to join the U.S. Marine Corps? How did the experience change you?

A: I had been working at the same job for a while when I thought I needed to start giving back. The biggest change for me was the ability to see something greater than myself; I got a real sense of the world going on outside of just my immediate, selfish surroundings. The Marines helped me to grow up a lot. They taught me the focus and discipline that helped get me where I am today.

Q: When did you decide to become a writer?

A: I've been writing all my life, but the first professional gig I ever had was a screenplay for Illya Salkind (*Superman* 1-3) back in 1995. But it was a secondary profession, with small assignments here and there, and it wasn't until around 2005 that I began to get serious.

Q: Has your military experience affected your writing?

A: Absolutely, especially the discipline I have obtained. Time management is key when working on projects, so you must be able to govern yourself. In regards to story, I've met and been with many different people, which enabled me to become a better storyteller through character.

Q: Describe your approach to the Bloodlines series. Did personal experiences in the military influence the stories?

A: Yes and no. I didn't have these types of experiences in the military, but the characters are based on real people I've encountered. And those scenarios are all real, just the characters we follow have been inserted into the time lines. I wanted the stories to fit into real history, real battles, but have characters we may not have heard of be the focus of those stories. I've tried to retell the truth of the battle with a small change in the players.

Q: Any future plans for the Bloodlines series?

A: There are so many battles through history that people don't know about. If they hadn't happened, the world would be a much different place! It's important to hear about these events. If we can learn from history, we can sidestep the mistakes we've made as we move forward.

ABOUT THE ILLUSTRATOR

FRITZ CASAS is a freelance illustrator for the internationally renowned creative studio Glass House Graphics, Inc. He lives in Manila, Philippines, where he enjoys watching movies, gaming, and playing his guitar.

A CALL TO ACTION

WORLD WAR II

BLOODLINES

A TIME FOR WAR

M. ZACHARY SHERMAN

KOREAN WAR

BLOODLINES

BLOOD BROTHERHOOD

M. ZACHARY SHERMAN

On June 6, 1944, Private First Class Michael Donovan and 13,000 U.S. Paratroopers fly toward their Drop Zone in enemy-occupied France. Their mission: capture the town of Carentan from the Germans and secure an operations base for Allied forces. Suddenly, the sky explodes, and their C-47 Skytrain is hit with anti-aircraft fire! Within moments, the troops exit the plane and plummet toward a deadly destination. On the ground, Donovan finds himself alone in the lion's den without a weapon. In order to survive, the rookie soldier must rely on his instincts and locate his platoon before time runs out.

On December 1, 1950, during the heart of the Korean War, Lieutenant Everett Donovan awakens in a mortar crater behind enemy lines. During the Battle of Chosin Reservoir, a mine explosion has killed his entire platoon of U.S. Marines. Shaken and shivering from the subzero temps, the lieutenant struggles to his feet and stands among the bodies of his fellow Devil Dogs. Suddenly, a shot rings out! Donovan falls to his knees and when he looks up, he's face to face with his Korean counterpart. Both men know the standoff will end in brotherhood or blood — and neither choice will come easily.

VIETNAM WAR

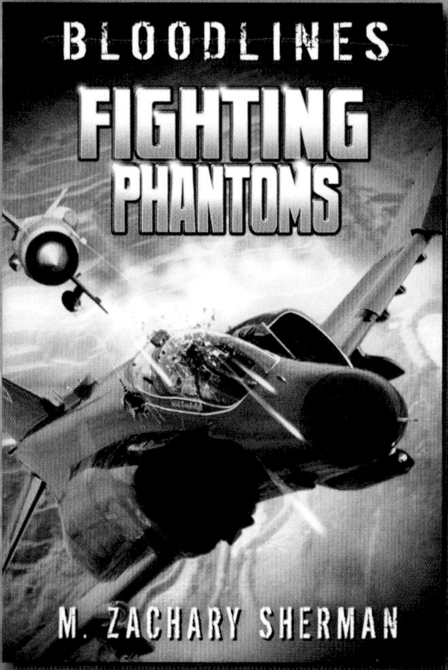
BLOODLINES
FIGHTING PHANTOMS
M. ZACHARY SHERMAN

In late 1970, Lieutenant Verner Donovan sits aboard an aircraft carrier, waiting to fly his F-4 Phantom II over Vietnam. He's the lead roll for the next hop and eager to help the U.S. troops on the ground. Suddenly, the call comes in — a Marine unit requires air support! Within moments, Donovan and other pilots are in their birds and into the skies. Soon, however, a dogfight with MiG fighter planes takes a turn for the worse, and the lieutenant ejects over enemy territory. His copilot is injured in the fall, and Donovan must make a difficult decision: to save his friend, he must first leave him behind.

AFGHANISTAN

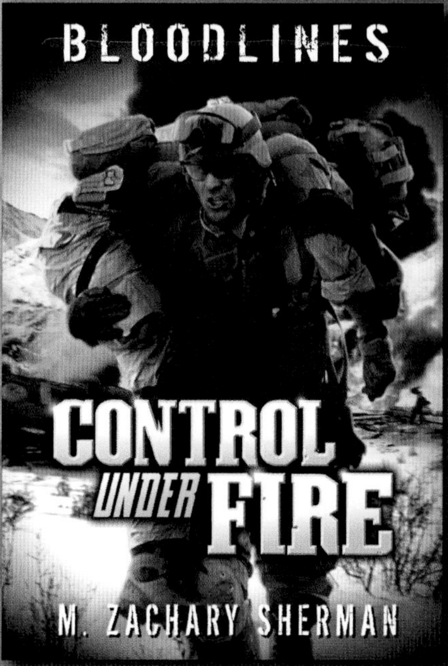
BLOODLINES
CONTROL UNDER FIRE
M. ZACHARY SHERMAN

Technology and air superiority equals success in modern warfare. But even during the War in Afghanistan, satellite recon and smart bombs cannot replace soldiers on the ground. When a SEAL team Seahawk helicopter goes down in the icy mountains of Kandahar, Lieutenant Commander Lester Donovan must make a difficult decision: follow orders or go "off mission" and save his fellow soldiers. With Taliban terrorists at every turn, neither decision will be easy. He'll need his instincts and some high-tech weaponry to get off of the hillside and back to base alive!

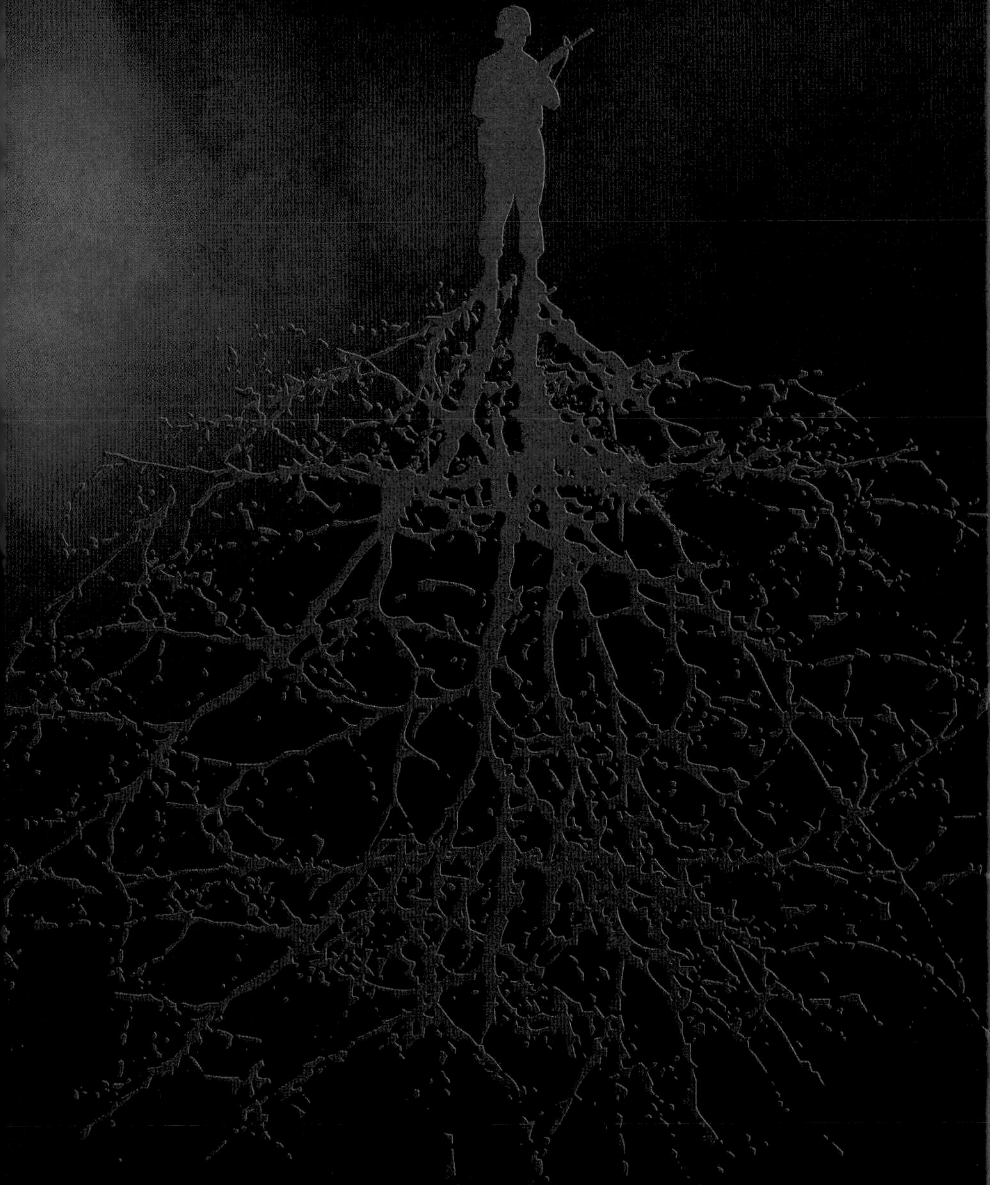

BLOODLINES

www.capstonepub.com